CYBER QUEST

Books by Sigmund Brouwer

Lightning on Ice Series
#1 Rebel Glory
#2 All-Star Pride
#3 Thunderbird Spirit
#4 Winter Hawk Star
#5 Blazer Drive
#6 Chief Honor

Short Cuts Series
#1 Snowboarding to the Extreme . . . Rippin'
#2 Mountain Biking to the Extreme . . . Cliff Dive
#3 Skydiving to the Extreme . . . 'Chute Roll
#4 Scuba Diving to the Extreme . . . Off the Wall

CyberQuest Series
#1 Pharaoh's Tomb
#2 Knight's Honor
#3 Pirate's Cross
#4 Outlaw's Gold
#5 Soldier's Aim
#6 Galilee Man

The Accidental Detectives Mystery Series

Winds of Light Medieval Adventures

Adult Books
Double Helix
Blood Ties

QUEST 4

OUTLAW'S GOLD

SIGMUND BROUWER

Thomas Nelson, Inc.
Nashville

To Jess, Morgan, Myka, & Myleah the wonderful Southern belles.

Outlaw's Gold
Quest 4 in the *CyberQuest* Series

Published in Nashville, Tennessee,
by Tommy Nelson™, a division of Thomas Nelson, Inc.

Managing Editor: Laura Minchew
Project Editor: Beverly Phillips
Cover illustration: Kevin Burke

Library of Congress Cataloging-in-Publication Data

Brouwer, Sigmund, 1959–
Outlaw's gold / Sigmund Brouwer.
p. cm. — (CyberQuest ; #4)
Summary: Mok continues his virtual reality mission in the old West, where he encounters a false preacher who is selling Pawnee children into servitude.
ISBN 0-8499-4037-0
[1. Science fiction. 2. Virtual reality—Fiction. 3. West (U.S.)—Fiction 4. Pawnee Indians—Fiction 5. Indians of North America—Fiction 6. Christian life—Fiction.] I. Title.
II. Series: Brouwer, Sigmund, 1959– CyberQuest ; #4.
PZ7.B799840u 1997
[Fic]—DC21 97-18212
CIP
AC

Printed in the United States of America

97 98 99 00 01 02 OPM 9 8 7 6 5 4 3 2 1

CYBERQUEST SERIES TERMS

BODYWRAP — a sheet of cloth that serves as clothing.

THE COMMITTEE — a group of people dedicated to making the world a better place.

MAINSIDE — any part of North America other than Old Newyork.

MINI-VIDCAM — a hidden video camera.

NETPHONE — a public telephone with a computer keypad. For a minimum charge, users can send e-mail through the Internet.

OLD NEWYORK — the bombed out island of Manhattan transformed into a colony for convicts and the poorest of the poor.

TECHNOCRAT — an upper-class person who can read, operate computers, and make much more money than a Welfaro.

'TRIC SHOOTER — an electric gun that fires enough voltage to stun its target.

VIDTRANS — video transmitters.

VIDWATCH — a watch with a minitelevision screen.

WATERMAN — a person who sells pure water.

WELFARO — a person living in the slums in Old Newyork.

THE GREAT WATER WARS—A.D. 2031. *In the year A.D. 2031 came the great Water Wars. The world's population had tripled during the previous thirty years. Worldwide demand for fresh, unpolluted water grew so strong that countries fought for control of water supplies. The war was longer and worse than any of the previous world wars. When it ended, there was a new world government, called the World United. The government was set up to distribute water among the world countries and to prevent any future wars. But it took its control too far.*

World United began to see itself as all important. After all, it had complete control of the world's limited water supplies. It began to make choices about who was "worthy" to receive water.

Very few people dared to object when World United denied water to criminals, the poor, and others it saw as undesirable. People were afraid of losing their own water if they spoke up.

One group, however, saw that the government's actions were wrong. These people dared to speak—Christians. They knew that only God should have control of their lives. They knew that they needed to stand up to the government for those who could not. Because of this, the government began to persecute the Christians and outlawed the Christian church. Some people gave up their beliefs to continue to receive an allotment of government water. Others refused and either joined underground churches or became hunted rebels, getting their water on the black market.

In North America, only one place was safe for the rebel Christians. The island of Old Newyork. The bombings of the great Water Wars had destroyed much of it, and the government used the entire island as a prison. The government did not care who else fled to the slums of those ancient street canyons.

Old Newyork grew in population. While most newcomers were criminals, some were these rebel Christians. Desperate for freedom, they entered this lion's den of lawlessness.

Limited water and supplies were sent from Mainside to Old Newyork, but some on Mainside said that any was too much to waste on the slums. When the issue came up at a World Senate meeting in 2049, it was decided that Old Newyork must be treated like a small country. It would have to provide something to the world in return for water and food.

When this new law went into effect, two things happened in the economy of this giant slum. First, work gangs began stripping steel from the skyscrapers. Anti-pollution laws on

Mainside made it expensive to manufacture new steel. Old steel, then, was traded for food and water.

Second, when a certain Mainside business genius got caught evading taxes in 2053, he was sent to Old Newyork. There he quickly saw a new business opportunity—slave labor.

Old Newyork was run by criminals and had no laws. Who was there to stop him from forcing people to work for him?

Within a couple of years, the giant slum was filled with bosses who made men, women, and children work at almost no pay. They produced clothing on giant sewing machines and assembled cheap computer products. Even boys and girls as young as seven years old worked up to twelve hours a day.

Christians in Old Newyork, of course, fought against this. But it was a battle the Christians lost over the years. Criminals and factory bosses used ruthless violence to control the slums.

Christianity was forced to become an underground movement in the slums. Education, too, disappeared. As did any medical care.

Into this world, Mok was born.

PROLOGUE

OLD NEWYORK—A.D. 2076. From a half block away, the ganglord saw the crowd gathered at the street corner ahead. He was a giant of a man, a fighter of many years. Beneath his protective leather pants and vest, his tough hide was covered with old scars. As was his shaved head. During his many years of fighting, each scar along the way had taught him something new. He had learned those lessons well. It had been years since anyone had dared to challenge him, years since he had been forced to fight.

And now someone dared to speak in public against the laws he, Zubluk, had set.

Squinting against the glare of the sun, Zubluk smiled grimly and touched the sword hanging at his side. Even though four of his men walked behind him—armed with spears and swords and crossbows—this appeared to be an occasion when the ganglord himself would enjoy dealing out the punishment.

As the ganglord and his bodyguards moved closer, they heard the old man's words.

"There is a truth," the old man was saying to the crowd. "It is a truth that will set you free from any earthly burden of pain or poverty or ganglord slavery."

Zubluk's grim smile became a frown. Dangerous as the old man's words were, there was also the matter of how loudly and clearly he spoke. Only electronic technology gave a voice that kind of power. Mainside technology. The man was not a Welfaro, for one of the slum dwellers would have immediately sold such technology for water.

What is a Mainsider doing in the slums? Zubluk wondered. The World United government did not permit anyone to cross the rivers back to Mainside. Ever. Taking a ferry into Old Newyork was always a one-way trip; the Mainside shores were guarded by land mines and soldiers who patrolled with dogs.

Zubluk was not stupid. No man reached his level of brutal power without brains. He knew Mainsiders also had other technology and weapons far more effective than swords or crossbows. And Zubluk had heard rumors of a man in the Scorpions' territory who had used an electric arc to defend a family from slavers.

Zubluk and his four men reached the edge of the crowd. The people's attention was directed forward on the old man and his words. The ganglord spun an old woman around, and she shrieked at the sight of his shaved head and scarred face. She put up her hands to block a blow.

"Bah," he said, and pushed her aside. He did not have time to waste on crushing insects when much bigger prey stood before him.

Her cry had drawn the attention of others, and the slum dwellers reacted in instant panic. Murmurs traveled ahead, like ripples of water from a dropped stone.

"Zubluk has arrived! Zubluk has arrived!"

The ganglord strode ahead, unafraid of the people massed around him and his men. No Welfaro had ever dared to fight a ganglord, let alone one with Zubluk's terrifying reputation.

Zubluk reached the front of the crowd. He got his first clear look at the old man.

In another time, the street corner where the old man stood had held a magnificent statue. It had guarded an entrance to a park and its lawn and trees and ponds with water fountains. Then came the great Water Wars. And in the aftermath of the wars were Technocrats and the World United government. No longer did people drive gasoline-powered vehicles. No longer was New York proud and free. Instead, it had become a giant slum prison called Old Newyork, where gangs reigned supreme and preyed upon weak Welfaros.

The magnificent statue had long since been pulled down for the value of its bronze. All that remained was its high, wide concrete base, stripped, too, of its bronze plaque. Behind it, the once beautiful park was filled with leaning shacks on littered paths. The fountains had been drained by people desperate for water. Abandoned skyscrapers with darkened, broken windows stood behind the park. Other buildings, bombed during the great Water Wars, had become gigantic heaps of rubble, like mountains overshadowing a village.

In those shadows where the statue once had been, the old man—Benjamin Rufus—now stood.

Zubluk did not know it, but twenty-four hours earlier, Benjamin Rufus had been one of the wealthiest and most powerful men on Mainside. Rufus had given up everything—name, fortune, freedom—just to come to this street corner.

He looked just like any other tired, old man fighting the heat in the Welfaro slums of Old Newyork. He was thin and stooped, his gray hair cropped short. Yet there was something in the old man's eyes—something rare in the slums. A joy. A peace. And no fear.

From where he stood on top of the statue base, the old man immediately saw the giant ganglord and his four bodyguards. Yet the old man's words did not falter.

"Look no further than your own love, fear, joy, and hatred," he said to the crowd in calm, slow words. "Look no further than the empty longing of your hearts. Surely these longings tell you that your body is more than just flesh. These longings let you know that you carry a soul. Let this knowledge then point you toward the God who breathed your soul into you. Let me tell you about his Son, who came into this world to save you."

"Silence!" roared Zubluk.

"You cannot silence truth," the old man answered.

"You can silence a man," Zubluk said. "You can rip his tongue from his head."

For a moment, Zubluk considered unsheathing his sword. But there was the matter of the dangerous Mainside technology. Zubluk's shrewdness outweighed his need to show bravery.

Zubluk waved his four massive bodyguards forward.

On the statue base, the old man smiled with a trace of weariness.

When the bodyguards were less than ten paces away from the old man, he pressed his elbow against his side. This released his 'tric shooter from a strap attached to his forearm, hidden beneath his coat. Without pausing, he lifted his arm and aimed at them, chest high. He pulled the trigger. In as little time as it took to move his arm from left to right, an arc of bright blue light swept across the four men. They crumpled with screams of agony.

Rufus brought the gun back to center and aimed it directly at Zubluk. But by then it was too late.

The giant warlord had stepped back into the crowd and grabbed a woman. He wrapped one massive arm around her shoulders and held her in front of him as a shield. With his other arm, he pressed the blade of a knife against her throat.

The old man's gun arm wavered.

"You'll never make a head shot from that distance," Zubluk snarled. "Drop it, or she dies."

The woman did not cry out in fear. She remained still, watchful.

"If she dies," Rufus said. "You lose your shield. I only stunned your bodyguards. But if you kill her,

I won't stop at stunning you. I'll stream the juice until you die too."

For several moments, there was silence. The great crowd had frozen.

"I know you," Zubluk said to Rufus, almost as if there were no woman, no knife, no 'tric shooter. "I have seen you before."

"Perhaps," Rufus said, "but it matters little. I have a message to bring to the people of Old Newyork."

"Not while I rule," Zubluk said. "I will hunt you down and—"

Zubluk broke off with a curse of pain as the woman snapped her head down and clamped her teeth on his wrist. She bit so hard that his blood streamed from her mouth. Then she twisted and pushed away from him.

Rufus took advantage of the confusion and streamed Zubluk. The crackling arc of bright blue light hit him squarely in the chest. With a single grunt, he fell first to his knees then face forward onto the ground.

The woman did not flee. She walked directly toward Benjamin Rufus. She was of medium height, dressed in rags, and smudged with dirt. A shawl covered most of her face, and it was difficult to see her age.

At the base of the statue, she reached up.

"Take my hand," she said to the old man. "Let me help you down. Then come with me. You will need someone to keep you safe here in the slums."

CHAPTER 1

MAINSIDE—TWENTY YEARS LATER (A.D. 2096). In a large room on the tenth floor of a luxury high-rise near the Hudson River, the members of the Committee had just gathered around a conference table.

A man named Cambridge stood at the front of the room near a gray vidscreen. He waited for the others to quiet.

With an almost hawklike face, he was tall and thin, his hair nearly white. Although he wore a cashmere sweater and blue jeans, nothing else about him was casual. As leader, the intensity in his eyes and his reputation set him apart from the other members of the Committee.

Cambridge turned his head slightly. It gave him a view through the window, a view of the distant slums of Old Newyork across the river.

The sight reminded him that those slums were the reason for their meeting.

The view also put another picture into his mind. A picture of the candidate named Mok, recently taken from those slums.

Mok was now motionless on a padded cot in a smaller room just down the hallway. Plastic tubes connected his body to a life-support machine. Other lines attached to his head ran to a nitrogen-cooled computer. Two nurses tended to the still body. Both watched the heart rate and other vital signs with great care. They had instructions to call a team of doctors and comtechs at the slightest sign of trouble.

Cambridge turned his mind back toward the meeting. He gazed up and down the conference table and waited for individual discussions to end. Cambridge felt a great sadness. He knew one of the Committee had betrayed their cause.

The room slowly grew quiet. Finally all eyes were on the tall man at the front.

"I would like us to begin with prayer," Cambridge said. "Our candidate nears the end of his cyberquest. And not one day too soon. All of you know how important the Senate vote is at the end of this month. The lines have been clearly drawn. We need Mok to swing one or two crucial votes in our direction."

"What is the candidate's chance of success?" asked one of the members.

"All I can tell you is what you already know," Cambridge said. "He has passed three stages. In Egypt, he showed that he believes in justice. The castle siege tested his beliefs. And he learned to testify with his growing faith on the pirate ship. His experience in the Wild West will help him prepare for the task he faces beyond."

There was a long pause. Everyone knew what was planned for Mok. But he had to survive these final stages. Otherwise, Old Newyork and its thousands of weary and helpless poor would lose all hope.

"Let us take this to our Lord in prayer," Cambridge said.

All twelve men bowed their heads. One, however, did not turn his mind and heart to prayer. His thoughts were turned to betrayal—and how to stop Mok. For he had been given his instructions by the president of the World United, the most powerful man alive. The words of prayer continued around him.

When Cambridge finished and opened his eyes, he felt more at peace. How important, he told himself, to look past trouble to the Father who waited beyond.

"You've seen the vidmonitor," Cambridge said as a way to break the silence. "You all know we have safely cybered Mok from the pirate ship to the western plains."

"Will the cyberassassin be able to follow him to the new site?" one of the Committee asked.

Cambridge fought an impulse to sigh. The reason they had left Mok on the pirate ship so long was to allow the comtechs to encrypt a new security code—in spite of the danger to Mok. They had to stop the assassin from following him through cyberspace. They had almost taken too long. The cyberassassin had been bringing his dagger down at Mok's chest as they pulled him from the cybersite. Another second and Mok would have died, for if a person dies in cyberspace, it scrambles his brain circuits and kills him in real time too.

"No," Cambridge said, hiding his irritation. "The new code is too complex to crack. Whoever managed to hack into our computer is now helpless to follow Mok."

"Excellent," another Committee member said. "The testing of our candidate can continue."

"It's good and bad," Cambridge answered. "Mok is safe, at least from the cyberassassin. But we still don't know who sent the assassin in, or how."

"Is that a problem? After all, the most important thing is the test," the same person said.

Cambridge shook his head to indicate a negative. "There is still the ultimate goal of the Committee. If we don't find out who was behind this betrayal, everything is at risk."

Cambridge cleared his throat. "And that means a change of plans."

All of the Committee members leaned forward.

"My full attention must be here," Cambridge said. "I won't be able to supervise Mok. We're sending the girl back in."

Excited babble broke out.

Cambridge raised his hand for quiet.

"Yes," he said, "I understand the difficulties. It means last-minute adjustments in the program. And she'll have to do the best she can in a dangerous situation. But we have no other choice."

Cambridge looked around and waited for any disagreement. None came. Cambridge ended the meeting. One by one, the members filed out of the room.

An hour later, Cambridge met with the senior Committee member and, as a safeguard against one person dying with the security access code to Mok's cybersite, gave the member the new security code. A half hour later, Cambridge called another Committee member and gave him another security code. By midnight, each Committee member knew a different code.

Only then was Cambridge satisfied to prepare himself for sleep. Whoever had betrayed the Committee was a desperate man. Cambridge prayed he had done everything he could to protect Mok.

CYBERSPACE—THE WILD WEST. The land around Mok brought back memories of his time in the desert of ancient Egypt. There the horizons had also stretched far in all directions, and the sun had been high in an endless sky.

Here, however, tall grass, not drifting sand, rippled before the wind. Here, the sun's heat was warm, not blazing. And here, the bronze-skinned man with a spear did not wear a tunic as the Egyptian palace guards had, but merely a cloth around his waist.

"Your brain is the size of a pea," Mok said in conversational tones to the man. "And your ugliness is only exceeded by your smelliness."

The man did not reply. He was on horseback. Mok followed on foot behind the horse. Twice Mok had tried to escape. The man had patiently ridden Mok down and jabbed him with the spear. Mok had quickly learned to follow.

Mok had also quickly learned the man did not speak. By Mok's estimation, they had traveled for two hours since the man had woken Mok by tickling his face with the feather attached to a spear. Not once in all those miles across empty land had this man answered any of Mok's questions. *Where were they? Who was he? Where were they going?*

After repeating his futile questions for the entire first hour, Mok had become convinced the man could not speak English. Either that, or he was deaf.

"Not only that," Mok said, looking for ways to amuse himself as they crossed the monotony of land, "but you dress like an idiot and people laugh at your belly button."

No reply, of course. Mok spent another five minutes insulting this man, then tired of the little game and fell into silence. It was broken only by the wailing of prairie wind, the sharp alarm whistles of small animals that scurried into holes in the ground, and the occasional piercing screams of hawks that circled the sky above.

Mok turned his thoughts back toward himself. Once, in another lifetime when he had lived in the street slums of Old Newyork, a man had trapped him in the tunnels and zapped a blue light into Mok's chest. Mok had woken, confused, in ancient Egypt. There he had survived an execution order, only to be sent in whirling blackness to a castle under siege in the Holy Lands. At the very moment of escape from that castle and the army around it, Mok had been rendered unconscious by a woman who had also been in ancient Egypt. He had awoken on a pirate ship. And during a mutiny aboard the pirate ship, Mok had faced certain death to a dagger held by . . .

Mok turned his mind to his final moments on the ship. There had been a giant savage of a man—

Barbarossa. The giant had called Mok a Welfaro. How was it that Barbarossa had known anything of Mok's life in Old Newyork? And by the giant's admission, he had been sent after Mok. *From where? By whom? And why?* Last, and most confusing of all, the giant had said something about Mok dying in two places. Had Mok somehow still been in Old Newyork at the same time he was on the pirate ship?

Barbarossa's dagger had plunged down at Mok's chest, yet Mok had not died. He had somehow been transported to starlit hills that overlooked a herd of huge, thundering beasts. By dawn, the beasts had gone, but Mok remained, asleep until this man on the horse had woken him.

Mok could not forget Barbarossa's words. *Two places?* Was that somehow the truth? Mok was here but not here? Then remained more questions. How? And most important, why?

How could Mok be here yet also in Old Newyork? Here, he felt the thud of his feet against land, the wind against his face. The bright sun made Mok's eyes water. He could reach down and touch the rough fabric of his shirt and pants. His legs were tired from constant walking, and his throat was dry. Here was as real as life had been in Old Newyork.

Here . . .

Mok wrinkled his nose.

The breeze brought a disgusting smell, a stench far worse than anything he had discovered in Old Newyork. And Old Newyork's rotting mounds of garbage had provided many unpleasant smells.

Mok looked past the silent man on horseback in front of him. Dozens and dozens of birds filled the sky beyond the next hill.

Five minutes later, Mok discovered why. He and the man on horseback crested the hill. Mok saw hundreds of huge animals—dead. The ground was stained brown from their blood. Mok remembered then that a thundering herd of animals had passed him in the night. Were these like those animals?

As they neared the animals, Mok could hardly breathe. Flies rose in clusters at Mok's shadow. He felt staggered by the waste of it all. Who had slaughtered these animals?

The bronze-skinned man half turned in the saddle and looked down on Mok. "It is your people who kill our buffalo in this manner," the man said. "They take only the hide and tongue and leave the rest. My anger is kindled against all with pale skin."

Buffalo. These animals were called—

Mok felt the flush of embarrassment fill his face. The man *did* speak English. He'd understood everything Mok had said.

"My name is Yellowbird Sings," the warrior said. "I am Pawnee. You are now a prisoner of my tribe. The elders will cast judgment upon you for these things your people do."

CHAPTER 3

A HALF HOUR LATER, Yellowbird Sings led Mok down a narrow trail into a valley folded between the hills. Halfway down, Mok saw large upside-down cones. As they got closer, he realized the cones were made of animal skins supported by poles tied together at the top. Smoke rose from the tops of these cones. From cooking fires inside?

Mok followed the man on horseback into the center of camp. The grass in the camp was well matted. Bones and pieces of hide littered the paths between the cone shelters, and the firepits overflowed with ashes. These people had camped here for some time.

As Mok walked, he watched the women and children as carefully as they watched him. Some of the mothers scraped at hides. Old women squatted near fires, stirring pots with sticks. Children clutched the women and peeked around their legs at Mok.

Despite the people that Mok could see, there was an eerie quiet to the camp. Then they came upon five dead men, all bronze-skinned like the man on horseback. All wore similar waist-clothes. All sprawled on the ground, clutching bottles.

Mok gasped at the sight. Then he understood they had not died, but passed out.

The man on horseback muttered something and climbed down. He shouted in a language that Mok could not understand. A woman hurried toward them. She wore a buckskin dress with fringes.

He spoke quickly to her.

She listened without interrupting. When the man finished his rapid-fire questions, she answered him.

Mok made little sense of her words, for she, too, spoke a language he could not understand. He heard one word clearly: whiskey.

She swept her arm and pointed beyond Mok and the bronze-skinned man.

Mok saw a large wagon, heaped with bloody hides.

Buffalo, he told himself. From the buffalo.

Two men dozed in the shade beneath the wagon. These were not bronze-skinned men barely clothed but grizzled, bearded men in long filthy coats.

The bronze-skinned man walked closer and jabbed at the men with his spear.

The two men roused themselves and rolled out from under the wagon.

Mok saw them closer. They were both short and pudgy. Both wore battered felt hats with holes in the brim. Their beards were crusty with the grease and caked dirt that also covered their filth-stiffened clothes.

"Hey, buck," one of the men said without any fear. "You haven't been in this camp for a few days, have you? I'll give you the rules. You want whiskey, go skin some of the buffalo we shot." He pantomimed to make his point as he spoke.

"Understand?" the other said. "No hides, no whiskey."

"I know what this firewater does to my people," the bronze-skinned man said. "You are not welcome at this camp. You will leave now."

"Is that so?" the one on the right said. He pulled a pistol out from under his coat. "How you going to make us leave? All I see on you is a spear."

The man on the left stepped forward and, without warning, punched the bronze-skinned man in the stomach. The one on the right hit him across the head with the butt of the pistol.

The bronze-skinned man fell. Both white men started kicking at his head and ribs.

Mok reacted without wondering why. He dove into both men, flailing with his arms.

Seconds later, Mok too was on the ground, blinking at the men above him. Mok stared directly into the dark holes of two pistols pointed at his forehead.

CHAPTER 4

"SHOOT HIM, JACK. Put some daylight into his skull."

"Let's throw him on a fire instead. Fool deserves it for taking the Pawnee's side against ours."

Mok flung himself away and banged squarely against the wagon wheel. The men grabbed him by the ankles and began dragging him. Mok tried kicking, but he was helpless.

Just as they reached the fire, Mok heard the thunder of rifle fire. Both his attackers froze.

From the ground, Mok saw the silhouette of another man on a horse.

"Get to your feet, son," the man said. "This is one man of the Lord who ain't afraid to use a Winchester to help preach the Good Word."

Mok got to his feet and dusted himself off.

"Now," the man with the rifle continued. "You two varmints drop your pistols and clear out. Otherwise there'll be plenty of daylight showing between your eyes. This Winchester don't miss."

The two whiskey traders dropped their guns and backed away.

The man surveyed the camp from his horse. He wore a black shirt, black pants, and black hat. He was a big man with a neatly trimmed goatee and dark, slicked-back hair.

"The name's Preacher John," he said. "What do folks call you?"

"Mok."

"Never laugh at a man's name, I say," Preacher John said. "Still, I got to wonder what was going through your folks' heads when they came up with that one."

Preacher John shook his head.

"Anyway, son," he said to Mok, "good thing I rode in when I did. Now let me ask you a question. Are you saved? And do you want to help me bring the Word to these Pawnees?"

"But . . ." Mok pointed at Yellowbird Sings just getting to his knees. "He said I was a prisoner of this tribe."

"*You* are," the preacher in black said. "As for me, I ride this land freely with the Word of God protecting me as I move among the tribes."

He smiled. "So let me ask you again. Will you help me bring the Word? Because if you won't, I'll hand you right back to those two varmits."

"I'll help," Mok said. After all, how could this possibly bring any harm?

CHAPTER 5

MAINSIDE. The man stood for a moment in front of a sink. Water ran from the tap over his hands. He felt no fear. At this late hour, the only other people who might walk into this washroom on the tenth floor of the high-rise building were security guards. The guards would recognize him instantly and leave him alone. They would not know his plan.

And, had any guard pushed the door open, it would have seemed, of course, as if the man were simply washing his hands. Instead, he was hardly aware of the water as he examined his face carefully.

He thought it was a wonderful face to have. By the time morning arrived, he would be on a private jet headed for Mexico, where he would have nothing for the rest of his life but sun, time, and money.

The mirror showed blond hair carefully brushed back in the latest Technocrat style. His teeth were shiny white and perfect—all capped of course. His nose was straight, his cheekbones high as current fashion dictated. Most Technocrats had plastic surgery at least once every ten years, and the reflection in the mirror showed the results of such care and attention.

These are the eyes of a man about to become very rich, he told himself. From the mirror, blue eyes gazed back at him in triumph. He winked at himself, laughed softly, and stepped away from the sink to dry his hands.

Moments later, he stepped into the quiet of the carpeted hallways. It did not take long to reach his destination. He stopped in front of the door. On the other side was the body of the candidate, held in suspended animation while his mind and senses traveled in the virtual reality of cyberspace.

He knew there were others inside the room with the candidate. Others who must be forced into sleep.

The man knelt in front of the door. He took a small plastic tube from his pocket. Squeezing it hard, his fingers broke the smaller tube inside. Immediately, chemicals began to mix in the tube.

He slipped the tube beneath the door. It was highly unlikely that either of the nurses inside would notice. At this late hour, they were probably fighting sleep anyway.

Thirty seconds was all it would take. The chemicals would burn through the plastic and release an invisible gas, consisting mainly of a chloral-hydrate base.

He would have preferred something with cyanide. It would kill everyone in the room without risk to himself. But his instructions had been precise: The male nurses were not to be killed. Once Mok was dead, he was to plug the machines in again. It would look like a natural death, and the nurses would take the blame for falling asleep on duty.

So it would be the chloral-hydrate mixture. A

single breath of it was enough to knock any person unconscious. In another five minutes, the gas would clear from the room through the ventilation ducts. But he would give himself extra time to be sure. He did not want to fall into the same trap he had just set for the nurses.

The man moved to the end of the hallway. He leaned against the wall as he watched the seconds tick by on his watch.

Exactly ten minutes later, he returned to the door. He had a key to enter. All of the Committee members did.

Quietly, quickly, he stepped inside.

He grinned in triumph at what he saw. Both nurses—big, solid men—were asleep on their chairs, heads dropped onto their chests.

And in the middle of the room was the candidate, lying still. A blanket covered him. Tubes ran from various parts of his body. The steady beep-beep of the heart monitor was the only sound in the room.

The man grinned wider. This was reason for more triumph. How difficult would it be to kill someone who lived only because of a life-support machine?

With a quick twist of his fingers, the man locked the door behind him. No sense in taking the slight chance that a security guard might stop by and check the room.

Satisfied that nothing would stop him now, the man stepped toward the body.

Blip! Blip! Blip! Blip!

As the killer with blond hair and a perfect face took his last few steps toward Mok's motionless body, the heart-rate monitor suddenly pulsed faster.

The killer stopped and cocked his head. His own heart began to race faster too. Could Mok actually know of his approaching death? Was his heart rate speeding up in sudden fear?

No matter, he told himself. It wasn't as if Mok could rise from the cot and fight back. He was in suspended animation and lying beneath a blanket.

Blip! Blip! Blip! Blip!

The killer then realized the heart-rate monitor showed Mok's excitement in cyberspace. He must have entered a new danger level. His heart—behind in this world—was reacting as if Mok's body were indeed where his mind believed it was.

Blip! Blip! Blip! Blip!

With a snort of laughter at his jumpiness, the killer squatted beside the life-support machines. He closed his hands around the first electrical cord plugged into the wall.

How simple. Just a yank of this cord and the one below, and Mok was dead.

Blip! Blip! Blip! Blip!

The killer wiggled the first cord loose. With a final snap, it pulled from the wall.

Instantly, the heart-rate monitor shut down.

All that remained was the final electrical cord. With Mok dead, the blond-haired man's dreams would come to life—while the dreams of the Committee died.

CHAPTER 6

CYBERSPACE. Mok stood beside the large wooden-spoked wheels of a wagon. Except for the strong odor of the mule harnessed just upwind of him, Mok had no complaints about his surroundings. A prairie breeze hardly more than riffled the waist-high grass beyond the wagon and Indian camp. Blue sky and horizon stretched as far as Mok could see in all directions with not a single cloud against the deep blue.

Mok smiled briefly, lifting his face to the sun and closing his eyes as he relaxed.

He had long given up on trying to believe his new life was some sort of dream. Like the hot sun on his face and the sounds of the Pawnee Indian camp on the other side of the wagon, the details around him were too vivid to be merely his imagination.

But Mok had not given up on trying to explain these events. Determined as he was to make sense of it, though, he had decided the only way to keep his sanity was to accept and survive each new world.

As Mok stood with the sun warming his face and chest, he realized with surprise he felt a degree of happiness. For the first time since he had been shot with the blue arc of light, he was not facing danger. No execution loomed at a pharaoh's command in this world. No castle siege or pirate assassin threatened him. This world, at least now that the buffalo hunters had gone, was calm. Enjoyable. And the wide sky and far horizon gave him a feeling of freedom.

"Son, how long do you intend to stand there and collect flies? We got ourselves a wagon to unload."

Mok opened his eyes. The man in the black shirt was standing in the wagon above, holding a sack of flour.

"Yes, sir," Mok said.

"Call me Preacher John. Or just John. But I've already told you that."

Preacher John threw down the sack of flour. Mok caught it with both arms and staggered under its weight.

It had only been a half hour since the preacher had saved Mok. In that short time, Mok had learned the man's full name was John Richards. He called himself a missionary and was known among all the tribes as the Great Helper.

As he had explained to Mok, he was just as interested in bringing earthly hope as he was in delivering the Word of God. Much of that earthly hope consisted of the contents of the wagon: blankets, used clothing, sacks of flour and sugar, and various medicines. Mok's job was to help unload this wagon. After Preacher John gave the Pawnee Indians the Word, Mok would help distribute the supplies among them.

Mok set the sack of flour down and straightened, just in time to catch another sack.

Men and women had begun to gather around them and the wagon, talking excitedly and smiling broad smiles. Supplies!

As Preacher John had explained, these Pawnee were supposed to receive monthly food and blankets from the government. But reservation agents were notorious thieves and passed on little of these necessary and often-promised supplies. Without the preacher and his efforts, the upcoming winter would be difficult.

Mok worked steadily. The pile of supplies on the ground grew higher as the wagon emptied. The Pawnees stood and waited as they watched Preacher John and Mok.

Mok was so intent on the steady rhythm of unloading that he didn't notice all talk around him had stopped.

"Son," Preacher John called down from the wagon, "I believe now is as good a time as any to see how much good you'll do me."

Mok wiped the sweat off his face and looked up at the preacher. All Mok saw was the outline of the big man, black against the sun. Preacher John tossed a small object at Mok, and he caught it more from reaction than thought.

"You'll be needing that," Preacher John said.

Mok studied the strange object in his hand. It was made of dark, gleaming metal. Heavy. Tube on one end. A handle on the other. It was like the objects the buffalo hunters had pointed at Mok's head.

Mok looked upward again, a question obvious on his face.

"Six bullets in that Colt .44," Preacher John said. He pointed. "And six braves waiting to see what you might do with it."

Mok turned his head to look. The crowd of Pawnee around them numbered at least fifty. All had frozen to silence. The crowd parted widely in the middle. Six tall, muscular braves walked through the crowd toward Mok and the wagon. All were armed with war spears, shields, and knives. All were painted with fierce expressions of anger.

"I expected this," Preacher John said. "Every group has its share of young troublemakers. I come to preach and give freely. Yet, they would rather take without first listening to the good Word."

Preacher John shook his head sadly. "Yes, sir. On occasion, some even have it in mind to scalp me and leave me for the buzzards."

CHAPTER 7

PREACHER JOHN hopped down from the wagon and stepped beside Mok.

"No one gets anything from Preacher John unless they listen to him preach," the big man in black said. "I've always found a way to stop the troublemakers myself. But I'm curious to see what you'll do. Being as you agreed to help and all."

The braves moved closer. They stopped twenty paces from Mok and Preacher John and the unloaded supplies. They stared at Mok and Preacher John in silence.

"You've got the Colt .44," Preacher John said. "Still, I don't advise you to shoot them. Makes it real tough to get the rest of the bunch to believe it when you tell them the part about how Jesus is love."

The warriors continued to stare. Ready for battle, they wore only flaps of cloth hanging from their waists. The lack of clothing showed that all six were heavily muscled. Their silence—and the unspoken threat of muscle—was more unnerving than any shouts of anger.

Mok stared back. He had no idea what to do.

Preacher John dug a small cigar from his shirt pocket. He put it in his mouth, lit a match by snapping the end against his thumbnail, and drew his first puff from the cigar.

"On the other hand," Preacher John said in an unworried drawl, "it don't do no good to let them just up and walk away with any of the supplies. Gives the others no reason to stick around and listen to the Word."

"Oh," Mok said.

The warriors began to advance slowly.

"By the way you're holding that .44," Preacher John said, "a person might think you'd never shot a pistol before. That ought to make things real interesting."

"You won't help?" Mok said.

"Want to see if you're worth keeping around," Preacher John said. He took another puff from his cigar.

Mok looked down at the Colt .44. He was gripping it by the barrel with his left hand. He put it into his right hand. His fingers fell naturally around the handle of the pistol.

The braves were only ten steps away.

The lead brave grunted something in a language Mok couldn't understand.

"He's saying he wants all the supplies," Preacher John translated. "He says step aside."

The warrior lifted his spear. He cocked it back as if he was going to hurl it at Mok's chest.

"This here is known as a showdown," Preacher John said. "I advise you to do something. These

Pawnee will lose a lot of respect for you, if I have to draw my other Colt and defend you."

Mok's mouth had turned dry. He couldn't even find enough moisture to swallow. The blade of the spear looked crusted with blood. It didn't take much imagination to see how easily it could impale Mok.

It crossed his mind to call himself an idiot for believing this new adventure might be peaceful and filled with freedom. Any second now, the warrior was going to throw that spear. And it would hurt.

Mok's fingers tightened with nervousness. His index finger caught on the trigger. An explosion rocked the air as the pistol seemed to jerk itself in his hand.

Mok looked down with disbelief. He'd never seen anything like this in the slums of Old Newyork.

Gunsmoke drifted up to his face.

Murmuring filled the air.

Mok looked back at the warrior with the spear. He was still standing, but he was staring down. There was a neat little hole in the lower section of the cloth that hung from his waist. The bullet had passed clean between his legs.

All the others in the crowd were pointing at that little hole and the daylight that shone through.

The warrior looked up at Mok. His face was puckered with a combination of disbelief and relief. He dropped his spear and put his hands up, as if begging Mok not to shoot again. The warrior stumbled as he began to back away.

The other Pawnee began to rock with laughter as the young warriors fled.

Preacher John patted Mok on the shoulders.

"Well," he said to Mok. "I suppose that's one way to run them off. Now let's get down to business."

CHAPTER 8

JOHN RICHARDS CLIMBED back onto the wagon and began to preach to the people gathered below him. He spoke Pawnee, which Mok could not follow.

Mok, at the side of the wagon, let his mind wander as he watched the men and women and children listen to Preacher John.

The Word. Preacher John had called it the Word. Preacher John was speaking the Word about the man named Jesus. Mok's thoughts spun back to the audiobook of his childhood.

The audiobook had been his most precious possession. It had spoken to Mok during the lonely, cold nights in Old Newyork while he hid in the tunnels from work gangs. From the audiobook, he'd heard about a man from Galilee, who promised a home for any who believed in him. The Galilee Man had given his life on a cross to save others. And, in the streets of Old Newyork, Mok had wondered again and again if the Galilee Man was legend or truth.

Until his adventure on the pirate ship, Mok had thought it nearly impossible that a man would give his life to save others. In Old Newyork, it was the opposite—too many often took lives to save their own. Yet on the pirate ship, Captain Falconer had said he was willing to die simply to save Mok and the prisoners on board.

Now, Mok was beginning to understand what a gift that sacrifice had been. It made him hungry to know even more about this Galilee Man. Mok looked forward to time alone with Preacher John to ask his questions.

It was late in the day and the sun cast long shadows when Preacher John stepped down from the wagon. Yet the Pawnee had waited patiently. Some of them had shown great interest in the preacher's words.

Preacher John waved the Pawnee forward. Then he and Mok handed out the supplies to families.

Occasionally, Preacher John would point at one of the young teenagers. There would follow a rapid discussion in Pawnee with the teenager's mother and father, accompanied by many hand gestures on the part of both Preacher John and the parents.

After this happened a fourth time, Mok stopped his efforts with the sacks of flour and turned to Preacher John.

"What are you discussing?" Mok asked. "And why with some families but not others?"

"Simple," Preacher John said. "I am inviting them to send their older children to the white man's school. I spent much of my preaching time to convince them that the only way they can survive in the white man's world is to have some of their children educated in the white man's way. The Pawnee need their own doctors and lawyers and teachers."

Preacher John wiped his brow. "See, son. Words just aren't enough. We have a call to feed the hungry and mend the sick. Once these Pawnee can help themselves, they'll be much better off."

Mok shook his head in admiration. He decided right there he would do his best to help this great man in his efforts.

It gave Mok new energy as he lifted and handed out supplies. He was nearing the bottom of the pile when he looked past the last few families in front of him.

He saw something that made him forget his sore back.

A few hundred paces away, a young Pawnee woman guided an older woman by the elbow as they walked slowly through camp.

It cannot be, Mok told himself. Yet it was. Although her hair was braided, and she wore leather buckskins, there could be no mistake. This was Raha, the pharaoh's daughter from ancient Egypt. She had also been Rachel, the servant girl in the castle. She seemed to be haunting him through time. All of Mok's doubts and uncertainties overwhelmed him again. What madness surrounded him? How could it be real that he was among a tribe of Pawnee, helping a great preacher?

At that moment, Mok only knew one thing. He must speak to the girl.

CHAPTER 9

HE FOUND HER at nightfall. She was brushing the long hair of an older Pawnee woman. Both were singing quietly near a fire.

"Who are you?" Mok asked without a wave of greeting.

He held his breath. The long shadows of dusk made it difficult to see any expression on her beautiful face. What if she replied in Pawnee? What if she pretended not to know him? What if it wasn't the woman who had dogged his footsteps from one world to another?

She did not reply.

"Who are you?" Mok asked again, this time with an edge to his voice.

Both women stopped singing. The older woman turned her head and spoke to the younger one. In Pawnee.

"I am Voice-in-the-Wind," the young woman finally said in English. "And my adopted grandmother says you have a rude manner of speaking if indeed you have approached me for courtship."

The older woman spoke again. The younger woman listened, then translated. A smile showed as she spoke.

"My adopted grandmother says, however, it may be worth my while to listen to a man of such handsomeness, if only he can be trained to speak more gently."

"You speak Pawnee to her and English to me," Mok said, trying to ignore the flush of embarrassment he could feel hot on his face. "How is it you know my language?"

"I have been sent," she said simply. "For you."

If she had slapped him across the face, it would have had only half the effect of her words.

"Sent?" he sputtered. "Who sent you? Why? From where?"

She continued to smile, but said nothing else.

"Please," Mok said. "You must help me. Were you with me in Egypt? At the castle?"

"Yes," she replied. "But I can tell you little more."

Again, questions flooded Mok. All the questions that had tormented him. She *was* the key. She had the answers. He fought the urge to shake her shoulders to force the truth from her.

"You know, then, what has happened to me? That I was born into the slums of Old Newyork?"

"Yes. But that world is more than 200 years in the future."

Each of her answers only spun more questions for him. He was almost dizzy with the confusion of what to ask next.

"Another has followed me too," he said, his words tumbling out. "Barbarossa, aboard the pirate ship. He tried to kill me. Tell me, please. Why has all of this happened to me?"

Voice-in-the-Wind smiled mysteriously. "All I can tell you is that I have been sent for you."

"Sent from where?" Mok tried again. He stepped closer. "Who sent you?"

She had the answers. All he needed to do was force them from her.

"I have been sent to warn you. John Richards is not what he appears to be. Tonight, watch him."

"Preacher John? He not only speaks of love, but he also shows it."

"Beware of false prophets," she replied, "who come to you in sheep's clothing. Inwardly they are ravenous wolves."

Each time she spoke, it was like a another blow. These very words had come from the Galilee Man.

"I had an audiobook as a child!" Mok said. "I listened to those very words."

"The audiobook is known as the New Testament," she explained. "It was no accident that you found it. For our plan was already in place before you were born."

"Plan?" He almost fell to his knees to beg. "A plan in place for me before I was born? Please, tell me what you can."

"Watch the preacher tonight," she said. "And remember this: What will it profit a man if he gains the whole world and loses his soul?"

Again, words from the audiobook.

"Tell me," he pleaded. "How have I been sent from Old Newyork?"

"How?" she said. "Too often men ask how, when the important question is why."

"Why, then? Tell me, why?"

He reached across the short space between them and shook her shoulders.

The old woman barked out words in Pawnee. Mok ignored her.

"Why?" he repeated. "How can I make sense of this?"

"Whatever world you find yourself in," she said, "that is always the question. For isn't every life a quest?"

Mok's bewilderment began to turn to anger. Before he could speak, however, three warriors stepped into sight. They pointed their war spears at Mok.

He stepped away from Voice-in-the-Wind.

"You will not see me here again," she said. "But remember my words. Watch the preacher. And take heart. The messenger is not the message."

Voice-in-the-Wind took the old woman's hand. With great dignity, they both walked away.

Mok glared at the warriors, so confused and frustrated that he would have welcomed a fight. They, however, seemed to remember the lesson that Mok had taught earlier with his Colt .44. They followed the two women and left Mok standing alone—with only haunting questions as company.

MAINSIDE. Silence had replaced the steady blip-blip-blip of the heart-rate monitor. Mok's heart was still beating, of course. But the monitor was dead. Just like Mok would be in minutes.

The killer was crouched beside the wall. His ears adjusted to the new silence. He heard the snoring of the male nurses in their chairs. He heard the plop-plop of liquids in the tubes attached to Mok's arms. He heard a gentle whoosh-whoosh of the life-support machine as it pumped air through Mok's lungs.

The whoosh-whoosh wouldn't last long. Once the killer pulled the final cord from the wall, the life-support machine would also shut down.

He reached for the cord. Wiggle, wiggle. The killer grunted with the effort it took to pull the big plug.

It popped loose.

The killer expected new silence. Instead, the life-support machine continued its gentle whoosh-whoosh.

What was wrong?

The killer thought it through. He decided the life-support machine had a backup battery system. The Committee wouldn't risk letting a candidate die in cyberspace by not being prepared for a power outage.

The killer moved to the back of the machine. He studied the wires. It took him a short while to figure it out. Then, with no hesitation, he pulled two other cords.

The machine stopped. As did Mok's lungs.

The killer clenched his right fist in triumph.

Dead, dead, dead. Mok was as good as dead.

Rich, rich, rich. The killer was now rich.

He backed away from the machine.

All he needed to do was wait a few minutes. Without the life-support machine, the body would starve for oxygen. No person could live without air for long.

The killer glanced at the door. The only thing that could go wrong now was an unexpected visit by the security guards.

One minute passed.

The snoring of the nurses continued as Mok's life slipped away.

Two minutes. Three.

Surely Mok was dead now, the killer told himself.

He forced himself to wait another few minutes. That time passed. All life on the table was gone. Without doubt. Absolutely. Positively.

The man slapped his hands together at a job well done. He replugged the cords into the back of the life-support machine. He plugged the other cords in place.

The life-support machine began moving Mok's lungs again. But the killer knew it was like pushing air into rubber balloons. Those lungs would never use oxygen again.

The heart-rate machine proved the killer right. It picked up no heartbeat at all. Mok had flat-lined.

Dead. Dead. Dead. Which meant he was rich, rich, rich.

The killer spun on his heels and walked with confidence toward the door. Once he was in the hallway, nobody could prove he had killed Mok. It looked as he had been instructed to make it look. It looked as if Mok had accidentally died as the nurses slept, not watching the monitors.

The killer pictured his walk down the hallway. His ride down the elevator. His walk through the quiet empty lobby to freedom. To the money he had been paid to kill Mok. To Mexico and a long retirement.

As he opened the door, he froze.

Four men stood in the hallway, two of them security guards. Before the killer could step back, one of the security guards pointed a 'tric shooter at his chest.

"This is set on kill," the guard said, "not stun. If you move, I pull the trigger."

The killer reacted with anger. "What kind of outrage is this! As one of the Committee, I have every right to be here."

"But not every right to unplug those machines." This speaker was white haired, the one named Cambridge. "The connections in there were set up to send instant alarms if the electrical current was ever broken."

The killer had stopped listening. He was staring beyond Cambridge at another Committee member.

One identical to him. Same hair. Same nose and cheekbones. Same perfect teeth.

That Committee member was staring back at the killer with horrid fascination.

"Cambridge!" the Committee member said. "This man is my double!"

"So it seems," Cambridge said calmly. "But should we be surprised? With a three-D computer scan of a photograph to work from and enough time, even the poorest plastic surgeon can remake a face."

Cambridge continued to speak as if the killer didn't exist. As if Mok had not been murdered.

"This shows that whoever sent him has been planning against us for some time," Cambridge said. "And planning well. If we hadn't caught him, the video monitors would have shown it was you in the room."

"Me?" The Committee member visibly sagged. "You would have thought I was the betrayer?"

"Stimpson, my friend," Cambridge said. "Even had I seen it on camera, I would have had difficulty believing it."

Cambridge half turned his head and spoke to the security guards. "Take this man away. We will question him later. I doubt we will learn anything about who sent him, but the effort must be made."

Cambridge fixed his eyes on the killer. A hired man who had let his face be shaped to match a photograph.

"I do not know what decisions you have made in life to bring you to this desperate place of greed,"

Cambridge said. "But there is still hope for your conscience."

"I don't understand," the killer said.

"In there," Cambridge answered, pointing, "you did not take a human life. Much as those who sent you have planned, so have we. Once the security code was breached, we took steps for what might be tried next. We set a trap of our own."

Cambridge smiled without humor. "Under the blanket lies a plastic dummy. Mok lives elsewhere."

CHAPTER 11

CYBERSPACE. Mok sat with his knees up and his arms wrapped around them. He shivered as he watched Preacher John's tent. Hot as it had been during the day, it seemed impossible the night could be as cold as the pinpricks of light from the stars above.

Mok would have much preferred to be wrapped in blankets. He could be sleeping, warm, under the wagon where Preacher John had sent him after the campfire had died.

Instead, he sat among low bushes. Preacher John's tent was only ten paces away. It glowed from a lantern inside. Mok guessed that the preacher was reading from the Word, as he called his Bible.

Outside in the cold, Mok was forced to endure the bites of mosquitoes, afraid to slap at them in case Preacher John heard him. Mok could only find consolation in thinking that between the cold and the mosquitoes, he would certainly not fall asleep.

More irritating than the cold and the mosquito bites, however, was the feeling that he was acting like a fool. After all, he was watching the tent only because of what Voice-in-the-Wind had told him. If indeed that was her name. In the land of sand, she had been Raha, the pharaoh's daughter. During the siege at the castle, she had been Rachel, a servant girl.

From a distant hill, a coyote began to wail. A coyote on another hill answered in the same high-pitched yipping. Mok shivered more, this time not from cold. The sound was eerie, but in this new prairie life, he had no idea if it was a sound of danger.

Mok heard rustling in the grass as mice and other small animals scurried through their night activities. Already he had heard a whoosh and seen the shadow of an owl against the moon as it swooped down and took its prey from those rustling creatures.

Again, he wondered about the many questions that had been with him since speaking to Voice-in-the-Wind only hours earlier.

She had been sent to warn him. She knew he came from Old Newyork—more than 200 years in the future. She had not been surprised to hear that Barbarossa, who had tried to kill him on the pirate ship, had also known of Old Newyork. It was as if both had been sent through time to follow him.

Mok blinked. He heard his last thought echo through his head.

It was as if both had been sent through time to follow him.

Could that be it? Could that somehow be the answer to all the mysteries that surrounded him?

In the beginning, there had been a man in the tunnel beneath the streets of Old Newyork. The man had shot blue light into Mok's chest. Instead of waking up in the slums, Mok had woken as a royal undertaker to the pharaoh.

Think hard, Mok told himself. *Think.*

Growing up in the slums, he'd heard story after story about Mainsiders. They had little boxes to speak into that could send their voices into other boxes across the world. There were the flashes of silver that crossed overhead with a roaring thunder that followed far behind. These giant tubes, if you wanted to believe the stories, carried Mainsiders through the air. There was the audiobook that Mok had had in childhood, a small box that spoke to him about the Galilee Man. The blue light he had been shot with, and how it had sent him into blackness, was surely from Mainside.

New thoughts tumbled over old thoughts so quickly that Mok had trouble staying with them. If it had been a Mainsider who had shot the blue light, then perhaps there were other Mainside things he could not understand. After all, if they could send their voices across the world and send their bodies through air, perhaps there was a device that also sent Mainsiders through time.

Mok left that thought in the back of his mind. He brought up other memories. What had the girl's last words been in the castle? *I'm sorry, but this was done to save you.* As if, perhaps, someone at the controls of a time device had reason to move him elsewhere. Like to the pirate ship, where he'd found himself immediately afterward.

And what had Barbarossa said on the pirate ship?

As soon as your head leaves your body, you will no longer exist. Here or there.

Here, as in wherever Mok had been sent. Or *there*, as in back at the device that moved a person through time.

Yes, he told himself with growing excitement. A device that sent him through time! This explained it! It wasn't all a dream. In dreams, a person did not bleed when hit or feel cold and bruises and hunger. In dreams, a person could not make up all the things and wonders that Mok had seen. But if he were actually traveling through time into different lands, it all made sense.

Yes! The dwarf named Blake, who had given him advice in Egypt and at the castle, had appeared and disappeared at will. Voice-in-the-Wind had done the same. And Barbarossa. They must all be Mainsiders, all able to travel through time.

Mok grinned in the darkness. This new answer, of course, led to other questions. Like why had Mok been taken to the Mainsider time device? And why was he being moved from place to place? After all, he'd rescued the pharaoh's daughter. It would have been nice to stay and accept her reward, in any manner she decided to give it to him. It would have been wonderful, too, to have remained with Count Reynald and his family as the son of an important man. Even among the pirates, if his new friend Captain Falconer had not died, Mok could have made a life much better than any he'd had in the slums.

Still, Mok felt a definite triumph. He'd found a

way to explain the insanity. All he had to do now was live through whatever—

Mok instantly shifted his attention to a dark figure moving toward Preacher John's tent. The figure called out in a low voice, words Mok could not hear.

The tent flap lifted as Preacher John invited the visitor inside. In the brief moment before the tent flap fell again, a flood of light outlined Yellowbird Sings, the Pawnee warrior who had found Mok alone in the vast prairies.

Was this why Voice-in-the-Wind had told Mok to watch the preacher? Was he going somewhere with Yellowbird Sings?

Mok waited, holding his breath to hear better. A murmur of voices reached him. But neither man stepped out of the tent again.

Mok quietly got to his feet. He pushed branches of the bush aside as he moved toward the tent. Moments later, he was crouched beside the tent, listening.

CHAPTER 12

ALTHOUGH HE WAS close enough to hear their words distinctly, Mok could not make sense of their conversation. They spoke Pawnee. He had just decided it would be wise to move away from the tent when they switched to English.

"Enough talk in your tongue," Preacher John said. "For this discussion, we speak English. It's safer. You're the only Pawnee in this camp who speaks English. We can be overheard, and it will not cost us our lives."

"What about the one named Mok? He speaks English."

"Strange name, but I like him," Preacher John said. "He is strong. He is brave. He is smart. I have decided to keep him as a helper."

"What?" Yellowbird Sings said. Angry. "You promised me gold for his capture."

Mok cocked his head. Gold for his capture?

"There is something about him," Preacher John said. "No fear. A sense of awareness. I believe it would be a shame to make him a slave."

Mok blinked. Had he heard right? A slave?

"But we made a deal. I deserve my money for him."

"No," Preacher John said. "He stays with me. It

won't take him long to learn Pawnee. He looks innocent. And from the sounds of it, he actually believes the Word. Someone like him will help us greatly as we go from camp to camp."

Mok's heart began to pound wildly. Something was wrong. Terribly wrong.

"But I should get something. You didn't have to put up with him on that long ride. Some of the things he said. That people laughed at my—"

"Enough," Preacher John barked. "This afternoon, the elders let me choose eight of their strongest young boys and girls. We leave tomorrow. In a few days, we'll have them at the mine. Then you'll get your fair share of gold."

Mok had heard enough to understand. Preacher John wasn't taking the Pawnee children to schools to educate them. He was selling them.

But how could Mok explain this to the Pawnee elders? The only people in camp who could translate Mok's English into Pawnee were Preacher John and Yellowbird Sings. He couldn't ask them to help him tell the elders.

There was Voice-in-the-Wind. She spoke English and Pawnee . . .

Mok straightened to move away from the tent. He would find her tepee in the darkness and tell her she had been right about Preacher John. She could warn the elders.

Mok took a step away from the tent. And tripped over a rope tied to a tent peg.

It might have been his grunt of pain. Or it might

have been the way the tent shook from the vibrating rope. Either way, it was enough to alert the two men inside.

As Mok scrambled to his feet, the men stepped out of the tent.

Preacher John leveled his pistol at Mok's stomach.

"It don't take much more brains than a fence post has to figure out you heard too much," Preacher John said. "Get inside the tent."

CHAPTER 13

THE TENT WAS easily big enough to stand in. Lantern light showed a folding cot, draped with blankets. A small luggage chest served as a table holding a box of bullets, a small oil can with a dirty cloth across the top, and a long-handled wire brush. Preacher John had taken off his black shirt. It was hanging from a rope stretched across the tent.

He stared at Mok, chest hairs curling from the neck of his dirty under shirt, his pants held by suspenders. Yellowbird Sings stood behind Preacher John, guarding the tent flap entrance.

"You impress me, boy," Preacher John told Mok, holding his pistol steady at Mok's belly. "It seems you had enough sense to know I wasn't a real preacher. And I've spent a long time fooling people."

Mok kept his chin steady. *The messenger is not the message,* Mok thought. *That's what Voice-in-the-Wind said. But what did she mean?*

"Thing is," Preacher John continued, "folks with less than admirable intentions often gravitate to thumping the Bible. People expect preacher's to be good, God-fearing folks. Those few of us who aren't find it easy to take advantage of that. Pretending to be a preacher is the best sheep's clothing a wolf can find."

Mok suddenly understood Voice-in-the-Wind's warning. Preacher John's heart was false, but the words he spoke were true. Mok decided to remember to pay attention to people's actions as well as listen to their words in the future.

He watched as Preacher John reached with his free hand to where his shirt hung. He took a cigar from its pocket. Without taking his eyes or pistol off Mok, he found his matches and lit the cigar.

"Look at you," Preacher John said. "I might put lead in your belly any second. Yet you ain't showed a scrap of fear."

Preacher John squinted at the cigar smoke drifting into his eyes. He reversed the pistol, and handed it butt first to Mok.

Mok's eyes widened with surprise. He was no pistol-shooting expert, but he had certainly learned already the power of pulling the trigger.

"That's right," Preacher John said. "Now you've got the draw on me. Do me a favor, and hear me out before you decide whether to plug me with holes."

Another long puff on the cigar. "I want you to join me," Preacher John said. "We'll be partners. I can make you a wealthy man."

"That's why you gave me the pistol?" Mok asked.

"The man holding the gun has no need to lie," he answered. "And I'm interested in what you truly have to say about my offer."

Preacher John grinned a handsome smile. "So what do you say? There's gold mines in the mountains where work bosses don't ask no questions about the workers I deliver. These Pawnee are easy pickings. I've been moving through this territory about a year now, and outlaw or not I already have enough gold to buy me a dozen mansions back East. And this ain't nothing the law gets too excited about. It was just a few years back a person could collect bounties on their scalps. In other words, this is easy money and no chance of jail time. Throw your hand in with me, and you'll never have to worry about money the rest of your life."

Mok didn't even need to consider it. He'd spent his life in Old Newyork dodging the work gangs. They often spread through the city looking for children to capture as factory slaves. And what he'd learned in his search for the Galilee Man was enough to tell him there were more important things than money. He had to remember no further than the audiobook of his childhood.

"Do not lay for yourself a treasure on earth where moths and rust consume," Mok said with a trace of a smile. "But lay up a treasure in heaven. Surely preacher, you know that."

Preacher John smiled back through his cigar smoke. "You really believe that Bible verse, son?"

Mok nodded.

"Enough to die for it?"

Mok shrugged and held up the pistol.

"That ain't much of an answer, son. You think I was dumb enough to give you a loaded gun?"

Preacher John used his cigar to point at the chest with the oil can, dirty cloth, and wire brush. "I was cleaning my pistol as I spoke with Yellowbird Sings here. When we heard you outside, I didn't stop to put the bullets back in. After all, more often than not, just the sight of a gun is enough to win a fight."

Preacher John grinned wide. "But putting the gun in your hand got you to speak honest like I wanted you to. Sad thing is, your answer just cost you a lifetime in the mines. My Pawnee friend will get his outlaw gold for capturing you after all."

Yellowbird Sings spoke from the tent flap. "We have trouble."

"What?" Preacher John said sharply.

"Warriors, maybe two dozen. Headed this way."

"Too many to fight," Preacher John said. "We'll hear them out. This boy won't be able to tell them a thing. He don't speak Pawnee."

"This is not good," Yellowbird Sings said softly, fear in his words. "They have two children with them. Pawnee children."

"What's wrong with that?"

"They are wearing clothing from the mine. John, they must be escaped slaves. Those elders have our game figured out. They will stake us to an ant pile in the morning sun."

Mok would have enjoyed spending more time watching the sheer terror that crossed Preacher John's face. But time was something he didn't have.

The tent began to spin with a blackness that was now becoming familiar. And Mok was gone.

MAINSIDE. Fear clutched at the Committee member so badly that he could hardly press his fingers against the numbers on his private vidphone. It gave the Committee member no satisfaction to look around his private home office and see the expensive art on the walls. Money had far less value when a man feared for his life.

After two tries, he managed to punch in the number correctly. Within seconds, a close-up of the face of the president of the World United appeared in the screen.

"Yes," the president snapped. The most powerful person among the billions who had survived the Water Wars did not have to be polite.

"Stage five, your Worldship," the Committee member whispered. "He has moved to stage five."

"What! You told me the candidate would be killed here in real time, that the life-support machine would be unplugged."

"It . . . it did not happen. Cambridge guessed we . . . I would be desperate enough to try something. He took precautions."

"Do not, I repeat, do not tell me that Cambridge

captured our man. It took a year for surgeons to get his face duplicated perfectly."

The Committee member remained miserably silent. It was answer enough for the president.

"You are a dead man," the president told the Committee member. "If this were an open line and half the world were listening, I would still make that threat. You . . . are . . . a . . . dead . . . man."

"Your Worldship, I can promise you that our candidate will fail. On my life, I make that promise."

The president glared into the vidscreen. "I've heard your promises before. Why should I believe you now?"

"I have the new security code," the Committee member said, almost stammering. "Our cyberassassin can follow him to the next cybersite."

"Don't call me until the candidate is dead," the president snarled. He hit a button on his end of the vidphone.

The Committee member sat staring at a blank screen.

CHAPTER 15

CYBERSPACE—PARIS. Cold.

That was Mok's first impression. Cold and gray of a winter twilight.

He stood on a sidewalk staring at old buildings built close together along the street. He wore black. Black pants. Black overcoat. Black mittens.

None of this surprised him. He had learned to expect the unexpected. Given time, he would learn where he was.

But he didn't know how much time he'd get.

Cresting the hill where the cobblestone street disappeared between the buildings, the first wave of soldiers swept toward him.

AUTHOR NOTE

Mok's story is actually two stories. One of the stories is described in this cyberepisode.

There is also a series story linking together all the CyberQuest books—the reason Mok has been sent into cyberspace. That story starts in Pharaoh's Tomb *(#1) and is completed in* Galilee Man *(#6). No matter where you start reading Mok's story, you can easily go back to any book in the series without feeling like you already know too much about how the series story will end.*

This series story takes place about a hundred years in the future. You will see that parts of Mok's world are dark and grim. Yet, in the end, this is a story of hope, the most important hope any of us can have. We, too, live in a world that at times can be dark and grim. During his cyberquest, Mok will see how Jesus Christ and his followers have made a difference over the ages.

Some of you may be reading this series after following Mok's adventures in Breakaway, *a Focus on the Family magazine for teen guys. Those magazine episodes were the inspiration for the CyberQuest series, and I would like to thank Michael Ross and Jesse Flores at* Breakaway *for all the fun we had working together. However, this series contains far more than the original stories—once I really started to explore Mok's world, it became obvious to me that there was too much of the story left to be told. So, if you're joining this adventure because of* Breakaway, *I think I can still promise you plenty of surprises.*

Last, thank you for sharing Mok's world with me. You are the ones who truly bring Mok and his friends and enemies to life.

From your friend,

Sigmund Brouwer

The adventure continues!

Join Mok during World War II in

QUEST 5

SOLDIER'S AIM

It's Paris during World War II,
and Nazi forces have occupied the city.
A group of resistance fighters secretly move
Jews to England to save them from the Nazis.
Mok finds himself in the middle of a plot
that could change modern history.